MeeMa's Memory Quilt

Treasured Stories of Watauga County History

Jane Wilson &
Michaele Haas

Parkway Publishers, Inc.
Boone, North Carolina

1999

Library of Congress Cataloging-in-Publication Data

Wilson, Jane, 1946-
    Meema's memory quilt: treasured stories of Watauga County history / Jane Wilson and Michaele Haas.
    p. cm.
SUMMARY: While spending the night with his grandmother, a young boy learns about the 150-year history of his home from a quilt that has squares depicting its special people and events.
    ISBN: 1-887905-18-9

    1. Watauga County (N.C.) -- History Juvenile fiction. [1. Watauga County (N.C.) -- History Fiction. 2. Grandmothers Fiction. 3. Quilts Fiction.] I. Haas, Michaele. II. Title.
PZ7.W69573 Me 1999
[E] -- dc 21   99-23795
                                                          CIP

Layout and editing by Julie Shissler
Cover and book design by Bill May, Jr.
Manufactured in China

Acknowledgements

MeeMa's Memory Quilt: Treasured Stories of Watauga County History is a project of the Boone Service League (BSL). It is designed to commemorate Watauga County's 150th birthday and to raise money for the Seby B. Jones Cancer Center at Watauga Medical Center. All those BSL members who had a hand in creating this book found it exciting to watch Watauga County history come to life through it. A heartfelt thanks goes out to the following people for their significant contributions to this project: The Boone Service League Book Committee; Charles Lentz and the Watauga County Board of Education Office; Kent Oehm; Ashley d'Ambrost; Camellia Ferguson; and the many friends and family members who helped generate ideas for the storyline. We thank Jane Wilson, co-author of the book, for her hours of research on the history of our wonderful county.

Finally, we would like to express our gratitude to all of the children and young adults in the county who submitted artwork for the book. Each one, whether selected or not, displayed such talent greatly exceeding our expectations.

Bibliography

John Preston Arthur, *A History of Watauga County, North Carolina* (Richmond, Everett Waddey Co., 1915)

A. Clyde Mast, *History of Watauga County, North Carolina* (Boone, North Carolina: no date)

Peggy Polson and Betty McFarland, *Sketches of Early Watauga* (Boone, North Carolina: American Association of University Women, Boone Branch, 1973)

Daniel J. Whitener, *History of Watauga County: A Souvenir of Watauga Centennial* (Boone, North Carolina: 1949)

Lyn Froelich and the Drawing One Class, Caldwell Community College

"Mommy, look! What a big sign! What does it say?" Ryan asked as the car whizzed by a huge banner on a Watauga County road.

"It says, **HAPPY BIRTHDAY WATAUGA COUNTY**," Ryan's mother replied. "Each year, on January 27th, our county has a birthday. Our county is over 150 years old!"

"That's older than you are, Mommy!"

"Ryan, that's a lot older than your MeeMa and Pappaw!"

"Will the county have a birthday cake?" Ryan hoped so because he sure loved cake...especially the icing!

"I think there will be lots of cake this year," said his mother, "because so many places in our county are celebrating special birthdays. And speaking of birthdays, ask MeeMa to show you the gift she received last weekend for hers."

Ryan saw MeeMa's and Pappaw's house up ahead, and he could hardly sit still. He loved going to visit and tonight he was even going to spend the night.

"MeeMa! MeeMa!" Ryan called as he rushed through the door. "Can I see your special birthday present?"

"Birthday present?" MeeMa said, as she gave Ryan a big hello hug.

"Ryan and I saw the Watauga County birthday banner on our drive over," Ryan's mother replied. "I told him that you received a special gift for your birthday and I'm sure he'll enjoy all of the stories that go with it. You two have fun and I'll see you tomorrow!" Mother got back into the car, waved goodbye, and drove away.

"I can't wait to see what it is, MeeMa," Ryan exclaimed, "and I always love your stories!"

MeeMa led him into the kitchen where the smell of homemade chicken soup filled the air. "I promise to show you my gift, but first, let's have some lunch!"

She didn't have to ask him twice!

Cherokee Indian

Will Huffman, Fourth Grade, Hardin Park School

As the last lunch dish was put away, snow began to fall. MeeMa kindled a blaze in the den's fireplace and went into the back bedroom to retrieve the mystery gift. When she returned, all Ryan saw was a 'plain ole quilt.' As MeeMa spread the quilt out over him, though, Ryan noticed that it wasn't plain at all.

"Wow! Look at all of these pictures, MeeMa! I've never seen a quilt like this one before!"

"There isn't another quilt like this one, Ryan," MeeMa told him proudly. "That's why I think it's so special. I've been quilting with the same group of friends for over forty years and this is one that we've been working on, off and on, for about five years. They gave it to me last weekend for my birthday and I felt very honored."

They both stared in silence at the quilt before them and then MeeMa pointed to the first square. "Each picture on this quilt has a story that goes with it; a true story or memory about our home...Watauga County."

"Ryan, this Indian figure represents the Cherokee Indians who were the first people ever to live in Watauga County. We know they were here because stone tools, arrowheads, and bits of their pottery have been found in many different parts of our county."

Spangenberg - First Recorded Visitor

Lindley Sharp, Senior, Watauga High School

"What story does this one tell?" asked Ryan, pointing to a square quilted with a pattern of mountains and a horse.

"It's about the first recorded visit to Watauga County by an explorer. Bishop Spangenberg came looking for some land to claim. He and his group took the wrong path and ended up climbing mountains so steep that they sometimes had to crawl on their hands and knees! Their baggage and saddles had to be pulled up behind them and their frightened horses had to be blindfolded and pulled up the mountain, as well."

"Can you take me to see that steep mountain, MeeMa?"

MeeMa sat back in her rocker and picked up her knitting. "We go to that mountain a lot, Ryan, only now it doesn't seem so steep. It's called Flat Top Mountain and it's where the Moses Cone Mansion is today."

"Was that where Bishop....Spankenburger lived?" asked Ryan.

"It's Spangenberg," MeeMa corrected, "and no, he didn't end up claiming any land here, but he did keep good notes while on his journey. That's how we know about him."

"Then who lived in the big house?" Ryan wanted to know, snuggling up underneath the quilt.

"Mr. and Mrs. Moses Cone," MeeMa responded, "but they just lived there during the summer. Mr. Cone was a wealthy business owner from Greensboro. He was known as 'the Denim King' because his company made so much denim, the material your blue jeans are made of. But he was very important to Watauga County, too, because he gave so many people a job helping take care of his house. He had a large dairy, apple orchards, gardens — there was a lot of work to do."

"There's still a lot to do there, but it's fun stuff, MeeMa. You can ride bikes, walk around the lake, hike, and you can even ride horses!"

"You're right, Ryan, we are very fortunate that the Cone Mansion has been preserved so that everyone can still enjoy its beauty," Ryan's grandmother pointed out.

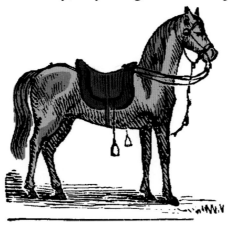

Daniel Boone

Justin Danner, Fifth Grade, Mabel School

"Is this a picture of Daniel Boone?" Ryan asked as he pointed to a man in a coonskin hat.

"Yes. That's Daniel," answered MeeMa. "He was the next visitor we know about after Bishop Spangenberg."

"I know about Daniel. I've seen the *Horn in the West*."

"I used to take your mother to see that when she was a little girl. The outdoor drama still does a wonderful job telling about ol' Daniel and a lot of people still come up here to see it year after year."

"Was the town of Boone named after Daniel, MeeMa?"

"Yes, in a round-about way," MeeMa said as she got up to check the fire. "Do you see the picture of a man who looks like he's hiding? There are also men with guns in the picture."

Ryan searched the quilt for the square his grandmother had described. "Here it is," he declared.

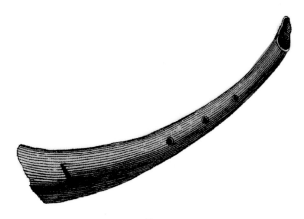

Howard's Knob Tale

Taylor Christian, Fourth Grade, Mountain Pathways Montessori School

    "The man who is hiding is Benjamin Howard. He lived down the mountain, in Wilkes County, and he used to herd his cattle up here in the summer to pasture where it was cool. He built a cabin for himself and his men to stay in while they were here ... it used to be located near Newland Hall, one of the dormitories on the Appalachian State University campus. Daniel stayed there quite often while passing through our area, and it became known as the Boone Cabin. Then, when Boone became a town, in 1872, they took the name from that cabin."

    "Why is Mr. Howard hiding?" asked Ryan.

    "Well, if you remember from The *Horn in the West*, many of the first people who came to America wanted to get away from the King of England and his rule. Mr. Howard, however, was a 'Tory' — which meant he was still loyal to the King. So, during a time in our history, called the American Revolution, there was a lot of fighting going on between those who wanted to be ruled by themselves and those who wanted England to control America. When they came looking for a fight from Mr. Howard, he hid out on the mountain north of Boone. We still call that mountain Howard's Knob today."

Cabin: Early Housing in Watauga County

Heather Ashline and Chris Ellison, Fourth Grade, Green Valley

"How about some hot chocolate?" MeeMa suggested.

While she was in the kitchen, Ryan closed his eyes and tried to imagine what life was like long ago.

When they had finished their cups of cocoa, Ryan pointed to another quilt square. "Is this a picture of the Boone Cabin?" he asked.

MeeMa picked up her knitting. "I guess it could be, but we just put a cabin on the quilt to represent the type of homes that were first built in our area. Samuel Hix and his family were the first to make their homes here in Watauga County, and they built cabins in Valle Crucis. They had plenty of logs to use, but no nails."

"How did they build houses without any nails?" Ryan's eyes were wide.

"They made pegs out of wood," MeeMa said, rocking steadily in her chair. "These pegs were like giant wooden nails,   and were used in houses, tables, beds, and anything else that they made out of wood. The floors in the cabins were hard packed dirt and a clay mixture, called mortar, was used between the logs and also for the rocks in the fireplace. The houses weren't big—usually one open room with a sleeping loft that you got to by climbing up pegs driven into the walls of the cabin."

MeeMa looked out the window at the falling snow. "We must have four inches already! If it keeps this up, your Pappaw won't make it home from his visit with Aunt Shirley in Asheville. I'll bet that church will be called off in the morning, too!"

Early Watauga County Church

Amanda Critcher, First Grade, Shepherd's Academy Home School

"MeeMa, did people go to church back then?" Ryan wondered.

"Oh yes," his grandmother answered. "Almost as soon as there were homes, the people were going to church."

MeeMa put her knitting down for a minute to look at the quilt.

"Do you see that church?" she said, pointing to a square on the side. "It represents the first churches built in our area. The Three Forks Baptist Church was the very first church to be built near Boone. Soon to follow was Cove Creek Baptist Church, built in the western part of the county."

"Were all of the churches Baptist?" asked Ryan.

"Yes," said MeeMa, "until Henson's Chapel Methodist Church in Vilas was built in 1866. Today, many different faiths are represented in Watauga County. But Three Forks Church was first."

First Schoolhouse

Shane DuVall, Fifth Grade, Valle Crucis

"What about school, MeeMa? Did they have *school* back then?"

"Believe it or not, Ryan, they did!" MeeMa replied, trying to hide a smile. "I'll tell you about the schools and then I'll let you help me start supper. Okay?"

Ryan rolled his eyes and nodded vigorously. He didn't want MeeMa to stop telling her stories, but his stomach was starting to growl.

"Okay," he agreed. "I'll help you cook after this last story."

"Well," MeeMa said, taking a deep breath, "where should I begin? The first schoolhouses were also made of logs up until 1900. That picture on the quilt is what a schoolhouse probably looked like then. Parents had to pay for each child to go to school until 1839, and then the state of North Carolina began to furnish money for schools like they do today."

"Did they have school buses?" asked Ryan, who loved to ride the bus.

"No. Everyone walked to school back then," MeeMa answered. "Guess what else? They had only one teacher for the whole school!"

"One teacher for everyone? I bet that was hard!"

"Well, Ryan, it probably was a little bit hard, but remember, there weren't nearly as many children in school then...not like today."

"I love my school, MeeMa. I love my teacher, too!"

"You're very lucky to be going to school in our county, Ryan. Our public and private schools and teachers are some of the best in the state! Once you graduate from Watauga High School, you even have a choice of colleges to attend right here at home: Caldwell Community College or Appalachian State University."

"I'm not even out of the first grade yet, MeeMa!" Ryan giggled.

"Yes, I know that, young man, but you're growing up awfully fast. You'll be in college much sooner than you think."

"See the picture of Yosef?" MeeMa asked Ryan, laying her knitting aside and standing up. "He is the mascot of Appalachian State University, which is over 100 years old. I'll tell you how the University got started ... *after* we eat supper." Hugging her grandson, MeeMa led Ryan to the kitchen.

Yosef -- Appalachian State University

Anne Tyler, Appalachian State University

"Ryan, I've never seen you eat so much! Does it take *that* much energy listening to my stories?"

"No," Ryan said, finishing his last bite. "It just takes smelling your fried chicken, mashed potatoes, and green beans!" He patted his full stomach.

"I'm glad you liked dinner. Now how about dessert?"

Ryan watched MeeMa take a pan of homemade brownies out of the oven. She cut a huge piece for Ryan, covering it with a scoop of vanilla ice cream.

Ryan didn't say a word, but his delighted face told the tale. He picked up his spoon and attacked the gooey chocolate dessert. Pleased, MeeMa began to tell him about Appalachian State University.

"Can you imagine what life was like without roads?" MeeMa asked Ryan. "It took a long time to go anywhere because you either had to walk or ride a horse."

"The horse part sounds fun!" Ryan said around a mouthful of brownie.

"Well, it is fun when you ride a few hours like you do now. But, imagine riding from here to Raleigh! It takes more than three hours in a car. Can you imagine how long it took back then on a horse?"

"Well, anyway," MeeMa went on, picking up the dinner dishes, "these two brothers, D. D. and B. B. Dougherty, had a great vision; they wanted to train people to become schoolteachers. This was over 100 years ago, so remember, Boone was only a very small village. They started out in an old building owned by their father, but soon B.B. started raising money to build a larger, newer one. Everyone pitched in to help. Their father donated six acres of land; Mr. Moses Cone gave money; and the rest of the community pitched in by helping to build it, donating building materials, or by giving money, too. By the way, did you get enough to eat?" asked MeeMa.

"I'm stuffed!" replied Ryan, wiping his mouth. "What about the horse?"

"I was getting to that," said MeeMa, taking Ryan's dessert dish to the sink.

Farming Scene

Erin Isaacs, Fifth Grade, Cove Creek

"When the new building was finished, it was called the Watauga Academy. Even though it was growing, money was needed to keep it running and to reach more people. So, on a cold, eight-degree morning, B. B. rode off on the family horse to Raleigh with a proposal in his pocket. He went to ask the government in Raleigh to make the Academy a state school so that the state could supply it with the money it needed to operate. The *bill,* as the proposal was called, passed by only **one** vote! It's kind of a miracle that Appalachian State University is even here!"

"Let's go check the fire, Ryan, it's getting chilly in here," MeeMa suggested, motioning for him to follow. While MeeMa laid another log across the coals of the fire, Ryan snuggled underneath the quilt again.

"What did people eat back then, MeeMa? Did they have fried chicken, too?" Ryan inquired.

"I think they probably did. In the early days, you only ate what you grew or hunted. At first they planted corn, rye, wheat, and potatoes. Then, as time went on, they started growing apples, cabbage, green beans, and other vegetables. They raised pigs and cows and other farm animals, and they also started growing lots and lots of tobacco to sell. Farming of tobacco and one other crop is still thriving in our county today. Do you know what that one other crop is, Ryan?" MeeMa asked her grandson. "Find the quilt square with the farm scene on it and then look for something that I haven't mentioned yet."

Ryan found the farm scene and studied it for a minute. "Are those Christmas trees, MeeMa?"

"They are indeed," she praised him, "it's the crop that our county grows and sells the most of today."

It was now dark outside and the snow continued to fall softly. Ryan felt so warm, inside and out; he snuggled deeper into the quilt. He and MeeMa had been contentedly sitting in silence for a while when MeeMa suddenly began to chuckle.

"What's so funny?" Ryan inquired. "Why are you laughing?"

Turkey Drive

Shaun Holder, Fourth Grade, Bethel

"I was thinking about that quilt square under your hand," MeeMa said, still amused.

"Are those turkeys?" Ryan asked, studying the picture.

"Yes. Those are turkeys and they're on a turkey drive," MeeMa said. "You've heard of a cattle drive, but could you imagine trying to herd a bunch of long, floppy-necked turkeys anywhere? When my friends and I were told this story, we knew it had to be included on our quilt. Partly because it is history, but mostly because we thought it was so funny!"

"Where did they take the turkeys, MeeMa?" Ryan wanted to know.

"Well, Mr. Clyde A. Mast would buy turkeys from local farmers right before Thanksgiving and then herd them all the way to Tennessee to sell. Sometimes he had as many as six hundred! Someone had to walk in front and every now and then, drop a little corn for them to eat, a couple of men walked on each side, to keep them going in the right direction, and a wagon usually brought up the rear."

"Why did they take a wagon?" asked Ryan. "Why didn't they just ride a horse?"

"The wagon carried food for both the men and the turkeys," MeeMa said, amused. "It was a long, cold trip to Tennessee and if a turkey got tired, it got to ride in the wagon until it was rested."

Ryan began to laugh then. He could only imagine how funny that must have been to see! Giving a turkey a ride!

"Ryan?" MeeMa said reaching for the bottle on the table beside her. "Would you mind getting me a glass of water from the kitchen? It's time for me to take my medicine."

Ryan hopped up and quickly returned with a small glass of water. "Why are you taking medicine, MeeMa?" he asked in a concerned voice.

"When you get my age, Ryan, you need a little more help keeping all of your parts working, but I'm just taking this medicine to clear up my bronchitis. It's certainly nothing to worry about....now anyway."

"What do you mean by .... now?" Ryan said, looking puzzled.

Old Watauga Hospital

Harold Frazier III, Seventh Grade, Appalachian Christian School

"Medicine has come a long way since the beginning of Watauga County. It's come a long way since I was your age!" MeeMa told her grandson.

"Did people have doctors, like now?" asked Ryan.

"There were a few doctors at first, but the woman in each home did most of the doctoring on her own family, or called a friend to come and help. People used to die from things that we have cures for now, like smallpox, German measles, and even bronchitis." MeeMa paused for a moment and then added, "There weren't hospitals, so women even had their babies at home."

"Were you born at home, MeeMa?"

"Yes, I was, Ryan."

"Was Mommy born at home, too?" Ryan asked.

"No, your mother was born at the old Watauga Hospital. It began as a clinic in 1931 and became a hospital in 1948. It was in the building that is now Founder's Hall on the Appalachian State University campus. There is its picture on the quilt," MeeMa said, pointing.

"When was the hospital that I was born in built?" wondered Ryan.

"I think," MeeMa said, gazing into the fire, "that it was built in 1967 and it was a whole lot smaller then. It is now called the Watauga Medical Center and provides care to people in many different counties, not just Watauga. It's really been a blessing to our area because really sick folks used to have to travel to Charlotte or Winston-Salem just to see a heart specialist or receive cancer treatments. Now, we have a Heart Clinic and a Cancer Unit right here in the mountains. It's saved a lot of time, and a lot of lives!"

"We have some pretty nice doctors, too," Ryan announced. "I ought to know, 'cuz I've seen a lot of them!"

"You *have* had your fair share of accidents, but, luckily, we do have some of the finest doctors around who can handle just about anything!"

MeeMa put her knitting down and looked at Ryan. "When I was young, I used to work at the Blowing Rock Hospital—that's where I met your Pappaw."

"Did he work there, too?"

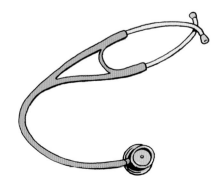

Tweetsie Railroad

Brandy Moore, Eighth Grade, Blowing Rock

"No," said MeeMa. "He was a patient, and a grumpy one at that. He moaned and whined, " MeeMa remembered aloud. "Looking back on it, he probably had kidney stones. They weren't sure what was wrong with him at the time."

Ryan didn't know what kidney stones were, but he bet that his Pappaw didn't think they were nearly as funny as MeeMa did.

"Then where did Pappaw work?" Ryan wanted to know.

"He farmed just like he does now," answered MeeMa. "He also earned some extra money by gathering barks, berries, roots and plants and selling them to local companies — companies that are still around today, I might add ... and then they re-sold them to larger companies who used them in medicines. But when your Pappaw was your age, he dreamed of being an Engineer for the Tweetsie Railroad!"

"That would have been great!" Ryan grinned. "I love going to Tweetsie — I'd like to drive a train too!"

"It was a bit different back then, Ryan," said MeeMa, "it was a real railroad and it opened up a whole new world for Watauga County!"

"What do you mean?" Ryan inquired.

"Well, we were known as a Lost Province," explained MeeMa. "We belonged to North Carolina, the State we live in, but we did most of our trading with Tennessee because the roads, or trails, were better in that direction. So, in 1917 East Tennessee and Western North Carolina Railroad was built to make traveling back and forth easier. People started calling it Tweetsie because of the sound of its whistle!"

"It doesn't go to Tennessee now....what happened?" Ryan wondered.

"There was a great flood in 1940 and it washed out most of the track," MeeMa recalled. "A man named Grover C. Robbins bought Engine #12, had three miles of track built, and started a theme park for our area. His wonderful idea has allowed millions of people to enjoy and remember the great Tweetsie Railroad."

Ryan couldn't quit yawning, and he knew it would soon be time for bed. He stared at the quilt and thought about all of the stories that MeeMa had told him. What a wonderful quilt MeeMa had ... and what a special county they both called home!

Ryan rubbed his eyes and started to lay his head down on the quilt when he noticed one last picture that MeeMa hadn't talked about. "MeeMa," Ryan said, "you left out one story...the one about these people ...who are they?"

Fishing: McKenzie Anderson, Seventh Grade
Floating: Kelly Walsh, Fifth Grade

Rock Climbing: David Harmon, Third Grade
Skiing: Katelyn Wells, Seventh Grade

Parkway School

"Oh yes, that one. They don't have names," MeeMa said quietly. "They represent what Watauga County is all about... people. Each year thousands and thousands of people visit our area. They come to ski in the winter. They come to hike, camp, fish, climb rocks and ride bikes in the spring, summer, and fall. They come to escape the heat and enjoy our cool summer breezes, and even to see our colorful trees in the fall. They come to shop, enjoy the arts and dine at our marvelous restaurants. They come to drive along our spectacular Blue Ridge Parkway or visit other attractions, like Grandfather Mountain and the Blowing Rock. The tourists, as we call these visitors, keep our county going ... tourism is our biggest business."

"If I didn't live here, I'd want to visit, too," Ryan confided drowsily, "but then I'd never want to leave!"

"That happens to a lot of folks," his grandmother replied. "Some people have come to our mountains to go to school or for a visit, and then decide to call it home. Others, like you and me, come from families that were here at the beginning of Watauga County."

MeeMa could see that Ryan was losing his battle to stay awake. "You know, Ryan," she said, gently taking his hand, "everyone who is lucky enough to live here has a big responsibility to our county... we must continue the quilt. We have to keep wise old traditions going and be courageous enough to start new ones. Each new day that we are blessed with is another chance to create some wonderful memories ... memories that could end up on another quilt many, many years from now."

Ryan smiled at that thought, but he was too sleepy to say a word. As he closed his eyes, he tried to imagine what pictures he would put on a quilt. A few came to his mind, but the only one that was for certain was this special day he had spent with MeeMa...MeeMa and her quilt of memories.

This page has been designed especially for you (or your family) to create, on paper, your own special quilt. How did your family, of different generations, contribute to your community? Remember, everyone contributes to the color of our world and has the opportunity to make their picture on the quilt of life a beautiful and unique one.

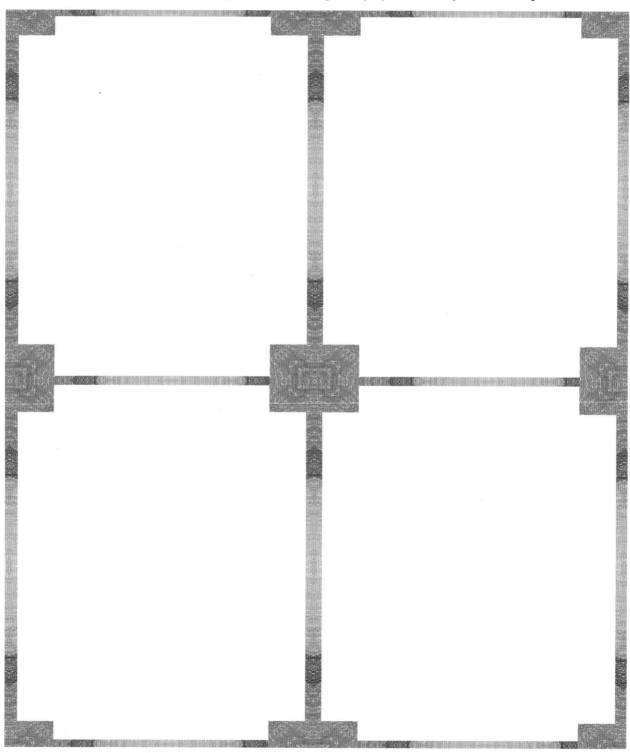